A Second Chance Brides
NOVELLA

The Widow
of St. Charles Avenue

GRACE HITCHCOCK

Published by Valmont House Publishers

GraceHitchcock.com

Names: Hitchcock, Grace, author.

Title: The Widow of St. Charles Avenue / Grace Hitchcock

Other Titles: the widow of st. charles avenue

Identifiers: ISBN 978-1-970675-01-6 Paperback

Subjects: Christian Romantic suspense fiction

All scripture quotations, unless otherwise noted, are taken from the King James Version of the Bible.

This book is a work of fiction. Names, characters, places, and incidents are either products of the author's imagination or used fictitiously. Any similarity to actual people, living or dead, organizations, and/or events is purely coincidental.

Cover design by *Valmont House Publishers*

Author is represented by The Steve Laube Agency

More From Grace Hitchcock:

Aprons and Veils Series:
The Finding of Miss Fairfield
The Pursuit of Miss Parish
The Enchanting of Miss Elliot
The Vanishing of Miss Victoria
The Courting of Miss Cady
The Making of Miss Matthews

Best Laid Plans Series:
To Catch a Coronet
To Kiss a Knight
To Win a Wager

American Royalty Series:
My Dear Miss Dupré
Her Darling Mr. Day
His Delightful Lady Delia

Heiresses of Adventure Series:
Miss Blaire in Blackwell's Island
Miss Wylde in the White City

Novellas:

Hearts of Gold, a Historical Romance Collection

"The Widow of St. Charles Avenue" in Second Chance Brides Collection

For Dakota,
My inspiration for all heroes.

"I am the bread of life. Whoever comes to me will never go hungry, and whoever believes in me will never be thirsty."

John 6:35 NIV

CHAPTER 1

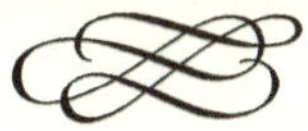

New Orleans, May 1895

"For goodness' sake, smile a little. You'll insult our hostess," her sister whispered, giving her a poke with her silk fan.

Colette Olivier pasted on a smile, hoping she appeared to be enjoying mingling with the other dinner guests.

Julia rolled her eyes. "Have you completely forgotten how to act? As the wife of Robert Olivier, you were one of the most influential socialites. What happened to your confidence and blasé demeanor?"

"It's been over a year and a half since I've

truly been out in society," Colette returned, smoothing the front of her blush frock, "so I'm a little out of practice." *And I was only a glowing socialite because Robert wanted me to be. If it were up to me, I would have stayed at home half the time with a good book and a cup of white tea,* she thought. "I wish I hadn't let you dress me in such a vibrant color. Did you see the looks I received at dinner? Honestly, I feel as if every lady in the room is judging me," Colette whispered, her pale cheeks turning warm. She tucked back a golden strand that had managed to escape her austere, high coiffure, which she was certain Julia would've altered as well if they hadn't run out of time. *At least the ladies might've thought my hairstyle befitting a widow, if only it didn't refuse to stay in place.*

"I know. I'm sorry I cajoled you out of your plum gown and into one of my own." She sighed. "Everyone knows that such a young widow isn't expected to complete the *full* two years in mourning. It's not as if you are shaming your husband's memory by accepting an invitation for a dinner party. The socialites are only upset because their daughters will have to compete with a rich widow for a husband sooner than anticipated."

Colette glanced up and saw yet another gentleman advancing to greet her now that her gown announced her return to society and the market.

"I'm beginning to understand some of the benefits of mourning colors. Do you want me to divert him?" Julia flicked open her fan.

"Please, divert away!"

"Mr. Carlson," her sister drawled as she grasped his arm and steered him in the opposite direction. "Have you tasted the pastries? Mrs. Lemoine's Italian chef makes a positively delectable cannoli."

Wishing with all her heart to blend into the room as she usually did, Colette poured herself a cup of coffee and, smiling to the hostess, sank into an armless chair in the farthest corner of the parlor. Closing her eyes to the fearsome glare of the older socialites, she inhaled the deep scent of chicory, praying for strength to make it through the rest of the evening.

"Why, Miss Fontaine! It's still Miss Fontaine, isn't it?" A deep voice broke her reverie.

Startled, she met the hazel eyes of her childhood friend Norman. "Mr. Hartley! What a pleasure." She stood and gave him a curtsy, careful not to spill her coffee. "But, I'm called Mrs. Robert Olivier now."

"*Mrs. Olivier?* Ah. Well, I can't say I'm surprised you were snatched up." He smiled, disappointment edging his words. "I haven't seen Robert in years. He and my father were friends back in their days at the university, so I know Father would be glad to hear of our meeting again. Where is old Robert anyway? Still stuck at the office?"

I knew I shouldn't have let Julia talk me into this dress. Anyone who saw me yesterday would've known not to ask. Longing for the comfort of her dark gown, she took a deep breath. "My husband passed almost two years ago. He was involved in a boating accident." At Norman's look of abject shock, she lifted her hand to halt his oncoming apology. "Please, don't be distressed in your inquiry. You happened to find me on my first attempt at attending a dinner party out of mourning colors." She laughed softly as she regarded the room. "But, I'm afraid, I may have startled some of the other ladies with my choice."

"I'm sorry if I caused you pain," he sighed as he raked his hands through his blond hair, "but I think it would've been a pity to deprive society of seeing you in such a sweet color that sets off those crystal-blue eyes I remember so well."

She felt her neck grow warm. It had been so many years since he'd left for New York that she'd forgotten how his flattery affected her. "You haven't changed a bit. You always were ready with a compliment. So, tell me, what brings you to New Orleans?"

"That would take a bit to explain. May I call on you? It's been far too long since we've last visited."

She glanced across the room at Julia, who gave her a small nod of encouragement as if she were reading Norman's lips. "I think it would be splendid." Colette smiled up at him, thinking how the past six years made him even more handsome as he had matured into a man. "How does afternoon tea next Saturday sound? Your aunt has my address."

"I'd be honored." Norman gave a little bow. "It'll be like old times."

A touch of mischief played at the corner of her lips. "In which case, I'll have the cook retrieve the pecans out of the storage pantry and make you some of those praline confections you loved so much as a boy." She caught sight of the whisking fans of the ladies in the corner with their heads together, chatting as they gawked in her direction.

Colette's stomach turned. *What am I thinking? I can't have a caller so soon.* She flicked open her fan to hide from the scrutiny of the other women. "I'm afraid I'm feeling a little tired and must fetch my sister home, but I look forward to continuing our conversation and hearing all of your news."

"And I yours. My mouth is already watering for those pralines." Norman reached for her gloved hand, pressing a kiss atop before she slipped away.

Wrapped in her cloak, Colette exhaled as

she and Julia leaned against the tufted leather seats of her carriage. "Thank goodness that's over."

"You were splendid," Julia gushed, giving a little clap. "Not that I'm a bit surprised. But *Norman Hartley* returns for not even a day and he already asks to call? To have that kind of talent to call upon. . ." She looked heavenward and inhaled. "I would be jealous if not for your history."

"Julia. . . ," she cautioned.

"What?" Julia raised her brows. "Norman was only twenty when he left for New York, and I distinctly remember him tearing up at our gate when he came to say good-bye. I was surprised he didn't marry you then and there and take you with him."

"While he did shed a tear, it was because we had been best friends since childhood." Colette smiled at the sweet memory as she stared out of the carriage window at the mansions on St. Charles Avenue, gaslights streaming through the windows.

Norman, her boy next door, had been the most eligible bachelor in New Orleans when she had first come out into society, but when he had moved to New York for business without asking for her hand in marriage, her parents gave up trying to match them. She had known long before her parents that while Norman may have liked her and maybe even loved her for a brief moment, he couldn't afford to marry a highborn girl who wouldn't raise his wealth with a significant inheritance. She'd understood then, and she wasn't about to become a romantic like Julia and envision a life with Norman now that their paths had crossed once again.

"He simply wishes to chat, so I won't have you getting your hopes up for anything more," she admonished Julia's enthusiasm. "I'm not that girl anymore who gets sweaty palms and a racing heart at the mere thought of Norman Hartley coming to call. I don't expect anything to come from it, and besides, he's probably seeing someone."

"I checked with his sister for you and he *isn't*. I'm so happy you're getting on with your life and receiving a caller. You are far too beautiful to let yourself wilt away in your widow's weeds." Julia grasped Colette's hands, squeezing them. "Now that you've captured the attention of the dazzling, wealthy Mr. Hartley at long last, you can help your baby sister find her own beau."

"Well, since I have my husband's fortune, I don't necessarily *need* to marry," Colette reminded her as the carriage rolled to a stop in front of the impressive Olivier estate.

"Why wouldn't you wish to remarry?" Julia twirled through the door with her hands clasped above her heart. "To love and be loved is all I could ever want in life."

"Just take care to fall in love with a man who can always keep you dressed in the latest of fashions," Colette teased as she pulled the tie from her cloak, glancing down at her borrowed gown. "Speaking of fashion, I'll need to make an appointment with the dressmaker for a new wardrobe." She handed her cloak to the maid, murmuring, "Thank you, Belinda."

Julia smirked at Colette's concession. "I knew you were ready to come back to society. All it took was a little bit of color to bring you to life and a beau to your parlor."

"I feel so strange attending social events

three months early. I fear what people will say." She rubbed her forehead. "Maybe I should wait on ordering those gowns."

Julia gave an unladylike growl of frustration as she kicked off her blue silk evening slippers. She carried them into the parlor, where she sank onto the red-and-gold settee as Colette chose Robert's old, oversize leather wingback chair. "People shouldn't judge you." Julia scowled. "You're too young to be so secluded from society."

"People will always judge a widow returning to society no matter her age, but I suppose you're right about getting out more. However, I don't want to be besieged with desperate bachelors who are fortune hunting. I'm not ready." She groaned as she, too, slipped off her shoes. Tucking her legs beneath her, she gazed into the glowing fireplace, which was lit more for ambiance than practicality in the warm New Orleans' night air. "I'm just thankful I can attend church without scorn. Those first few months after Robert's death were wretched, forced to being isolated and discouraged from even attending service."

"Hmm." Julia tapped her chin. "Well, what if you get involved in church as a means to ease into society again? You could volunteer as a Sunday school teacher or something of the sort. If I recall, you used to love working for charity and—" She left off her sentence as the maid rolled in the tea service. "Ah, lovely." Julia reached for the pot without waiting for Colette to formally do the honors and poured herself a cup, plunking four lumps of sugar into her tea. When the maid closed the door, she continued, "Why did you stop volunteering in the first place?"

Colette watched the steam curl as she slowly poured and considered revealing her secret. Leaning back, she took a long sip. "When Father presented me with Robert, I didn't allow myself to question if marrying an unbeliever was best because Father said it didn't matter. . .but it did. I should've prayed for guidance before I married Robert, but instead, I followed Father's advice without question." She looked down at her tea and swirled the dregs around in the cup. "My whole life I was told that as merely a woman, I wouldn't know what was best for my future and that I must listen, but I should've listened to the Lord."

"But, Robert wasn't harsh, was he?" Julia pressed her hand to her heart at the news of her sister's less-than-happy marriage.

"Robert was kind when we were courting, and because he thought me pretty, he didn't mind my small inheritance," she answered, stroking the handle of her teacup with her thumb, "but after we married, he became very strict. Things grew difficult when Robert stopped attending service. It created a barrier in our relationship, but I had hope that he'd eventually come with me again until one evening when I came home late from volunteering. Robert had made spontaneous plans for us to dine with a potential investor and his wife, which I ruined by not being home and not leaving a note letting him know where I was working that day. He was so angry that he forbade me from ever serving again."

Julia dropped her teacup in the saucer, sloshing its contents. "I didn't know. I thought you gave it up because you were too busy being a wife to Robert, and now to hear. . .no wonder you don't wish to marry again. Why did you wait so long to tell me?"

"Because I was ashamed," Colette admitted. "And I didn't return to my charity work after his death out of respect to his memory. I long to go back, but I still feel so trapped by his and society's disapproval. I never was good enough in their eyes for Robert and his fortune, and tonight probably solidified their opinion of me by my attempting to come out of mourning three months early." She took a sip of tea to steady her nerves. "But, maybe it's time I go against his wishes and volunteer again."

Julia reached out and gently squeezed her arm. "You should. Write to the pastor tonight and see what happens. If Norman doesn't cause your heart to pitter-patter anymore, which I doubt because the man is almost prettier than you, maybe you'll meet someone through the church who will steal your heart right out of your chest before you even know it's in danger."

THE DOORBELL RANG AGAIN. "BELINDA?" Colette called up the stairs as loud as she dared for fear of being overheard by the guest at the door. *Where is everyone? I need to dress for dinner.* After waiting another minute for the maid or butler to appear, she smoothed down any strands of escaped hair and opened the door herself.

A tall, ruggedly handsome man stood on the porch, and upon seeing Colette, he swiped off his hat, revealing his unruly auburn curls as he gave a small bow. "Good morning, ma'am. I'm Malcolm Reilly. Pastor Wilson mentioned you were keen on teaching Sunday school?"

"Uh, yes," she started, unsure of why he was asking.

He brandished a letter from his coat pocket. "This is from Mrs. Wilson, explaining why I am at your door."

Goodness, already? It's only been three days. "Yes, thank you." She accepted the letter. "I'm sorry. Where are my manners? Won't you come inside?" Colette asked, holding the door open.

He gestured to the clear blue sky. "It's a

beautiful day. Why don't we sit on the porch? I'd hate to trudge any dirt into your parlor. I came from the warehouse district, as I was out of the office today observing the workers and am not parlor friendly at the moment."

Colette's gaze fell on his filthy work boots. "Oh, yes. Please, do sit down." She stepped out onto the veranda and sank onto a wicker chair as she broke the sealed letter and scanned it. "You're the pastor's son?"

"Yes, ma'am," he replied as he rubbed the brim of his hat.

I wonder why he doesn't go by the same surname. Memories of the wild pastor's son dipping her curls in ink flooded her memory. Smiling at the recollection, she wondered if he knew that she was the victim of half a dozen of his antics as she motioned for him to continue. "Please, tell me about your Sunday school class."

"Well," he chuckled, "it's more of a Bible class since we meet on Friday afternoon because the children attend their own service on Sunday. I was hoping to find another teacher to help me restore order. The boys can get quite rowdy."

"Boys?" Her voice squeaked.

He grinned at her surprise, causing her heart to jump unexpectedly at the sight of his dimpled cheeks. "Yes, I teach the ten- to fourteen-year-old boys over at St. Mary's Orphanage. Mother left that out of the letter?"

"Ah." She inhaled through her teeth. "I had thought I'd be teaching the young ladies of the church as I'd have more to offer with my finishing school experience." She cleared her throat as she folded up the letter, disappointed that she wouldn't begin serving so soon after all.

He leaned forward in his chair. "You see, that's where I think you aren't giving yourself enough credit. Most of these boys only have the influence of their male teachers and a handful of nuns who work so hard that they don't have as much time as they'd like to nurture the boys. I believe you'll provide a calming presence and teach them how to behave in front of a lady, which"—he smiled—"the nuns will appreciate."

She gave a short, disbelieving laugh. *Either he has vastly overestimated my skills, or he is desperate, but I can't possibly work with a man. Mother would have an attack.* "Be that as it may—"

He held up a large, rough hand. "At least come with me one time on Friday before you turn it down altogether. I promise that when you meet these boys, you won't ever want to leave them."

She felt her resolution waver at his confidence. *Well, maybe just this once, and with the nuns present, I'm sure it'll be more than proper.* "What time shall I meet you?"

CHAPTER 2

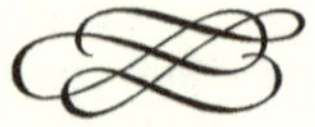

"Where are you going, Mr. Reilly?" Colette called to him as he passed the waiting carriage in front of her mansion.

"I thought we'd take the streetcar to the orphanage," Malcolm replied, shifting her heavy-laden basket of baked goods in his grip. "No sense in having your driver wait for over two hours while we give our first lesson together."

Colette swallowed at the thought of taking public transportation. Even though the St. Charles Avenue line had a stop steps from her drive, she had never needed to use it, and Robert would've never approved even if she had. "Is it, uh, quite safe?" she questioned, as she hadn't been on the new-fangled electric line yet since it was installed right before Robert's accident.

Malcolm laughed and offered her his elbow to cross the street. "It's much faster than the old bobtail line and safer, as we don't have to rely on the whims of the mules, but we can take a hired carriage back if you discover it is too much."

Waiting on the neutral ground, Colette judged the safety of the red streetcar as it screeched to a halt. Malcolm handed her the basket, stepped up to pay for their passage, and then extended his hand down to her. Stepping inside, she eyed the wooden seats, searching for a spot with the least amount of grime.

Malcolm's eyes laughed at her as he waited for her to choose a row before he took the seat opposite and set her basket of baked goods beside her. The streetcar jerked as it began rolling down the line, swaying with each turn of the wheel. She gripped the windowsill, grateful that all the windows seemed permanently lowered to allow the fresh, humid air, and not the scent of the passengers, to fill her lungs.

To distract herself from becoming sick from the motion, she attempted to break the awkward silence of being alone in public with a man she hadn't spoken to since she was a girl. "So, what caused you to become interested in teaching Sunday school to orphans, Mr. Reilly? Even if you are the son of a pastor, most young men I know are more interested in their horses, stocks, and planning their next hunting trips on their time off." *Besides, you were hardly pastoral when you were busy tying Theresa Ann's and my braids together in Sunday school class.*

Malcolm grinned, his dimples causing her heart to dip. "Well, it may help explain things in that I don't live on St. Charles Avenue or Royal Street as your acquaintances. I was raised at St. Mary's Orphanage until I was ten, when Mr. and Mrs. Wilson adopted me."

Attempting to conceal her shock in not recalling that rather sizable detail, she dropped her gaze and smoothed her dove-gray skirt, unsure of what to say next. "So that's why you serve at an orphanage?"

He nodded. "After I was adopted, we continued to serve at the orphanages weekly, and through my time under the Wilsons' wing, I realized education would be the only way of giving myself a fighting chance to make something of myself. Even though I'm now the son of a pastor, people still see me as the orphan waif of very low birth."

Colette wished she could negate his statement, but she knew society was ruthless in whom they accepted as worthy in their circles.

"Because of the many charities my parents supported, money was always tight, so when Miss Sophie Wright opened her free night school for young men, I was one of the first in attendance. In her classes, I began to dream of becoming a teacher to the lower classes, but as that required more training than I was receiving, I settled for working as one of the clerks in the shipping office until I can save enough money to attend college classes and earn my teacher's certificate."

Respect for this ambitious, generous man filled her. She knew socialites who wouldn't hesitate in dropping charity work if they had a spontaneous teatime to attend. Her cheeks warmed, knowing she had done the same more than once. The streetcar halted, jostling her chapeau, and she was grateful for the excuse to fidget as she repositioned her hat and gained control of her coloring, hoping he wouldn't notice her shame.

"We have to change lines here," Malcolm stated, extending his arm to her. "It's just a short walk."

When they had settled into their new streetcar, Colette pressed her handkerchief to her neck, patting away the perspiration from the "short" walk, before prompting him to continue his story. "So even with your working and saving for classes, you still find time for the orphans every Friday?"

He smiled, nodding. "About thirteen years ago, Margaret Gaffney Haughery, one of the only adults who cared about me before the Wilsons, passed away. Her husband and only child died in the yellow fever epidemic that left so many orphans. As a childless widow, she dedicated her fortune and life to taking care of the motherless children."

Her brows rose at the thought, and she couldn't help but ask, "And her remaining family supported her endeavor?"

He shrugged. "Probably not, but the children of New Orleans became her family. I like to carry on the tradition in honor of 'the bread lady,' as she fondly became known as to us orphans. She left her estate in the stewardship of the Daughters of Charity for the orphans of New Orleans, so her legacy lives on to this day."

Her heart clinched as envy filled her. *To be allowed to spend one's fortune without expectation.* "She sounds like quite the woman.

Not many would spend their life much less their money on such an endeavor."

"Mrs. Haughery was my guardian angel. I try to do as much as I can, but it's hard to make a difference when the people seem to have forgotten the plight of the orphans," Malcolm replied, rising as they had reached the end of the Dauphine Street line. "St. Mary's is two blocks south."

"But aren't there quite a few orphanages and homes in New Orleans with benefactors to provide for them?" Colette asked, knowing she attended at least one charity event a year devoted to benefiting the orphans. Feeling a slight breeze, Colette found herself across the street from the Mississippi River as they halted at the corner of Chartres and Mazant Streets in front of a large gray building.

Malcolm shrugged as he rang the bell. "There's always a need. No matter how many children are sheltered here, there's always more on the street."

The door creaked as it was wrenched open an inch by a pair of withered, spotted hands. "Yes?"

"Sister Joan?" He tucked his cap under his arm.

"My dear Malcolm! I couldn't remember if you were coming by today." She smiled, her forehead wrinkling beneath her wimple as she beckoned them into the hallway. She threaded her hands around Malcolm's muscular arm. "The children will be happy to see you as always." Her gaze fell on Colette's mauve chapeau and gray dress with its heavy lace, and understanding lit her features. "And who is your friend?"

"Sister Joan, may I present Mrs. Olivier? She's here to help me with the boys."

"Wonderful!" She patted Colette on the arm. "We can always use another pair of willing hands. If you'll follow us this way, Mrs. Olivier, we'll introduce you to the children."

Colette's heels clicked on the hardwood floors as she caught sight of the once glorious crown molding bowing away from the ceiling with small patches of mildew and watermarks trailing down from its cracks onto the wall. While the floors were spotless and the rooms kept tidy, the estate was in desperate need of funds.

Passing by an open door, she spotted a small boy standing on an overturned crate, peering through the windowpanes onto the street below with such a forlorn look on his little face that she had to pause. Lightly tugging on Malcolm's sleeve, she pointed to the dark-haired child. "Do you know him?"

Sister Joan leaned through the door to see what had caught Colette's interest. "Oh, that's Darvy. He turned seven last month and was transferred from one of the city's infant asylums."

"Transferred?"

"The infant asylum only keeps the children until they are seven. The girls have a specific orphanage they are released to, but the boys go to wherever there is an opening, regardless if they know anyone or not. There are always more orphans than space," Malcolm expounded before he crossed the room and crouched down by the lad.

Colette stiffened in the door frame, hesitant of what to do, for she had no experience with crying children.

"Hello there." Malcolm extended his hand as if greeting a man. "It's Darvy, isn't it? What's wrong?"

The child turned his attention to Malcolm and gave a hesitant nod as he sniffed back a tear and accepted Malcolm's handshake. "I miss Mary. They said she couldn't come here."

Malcolm wiped away a rolling tear and placed a hand on Darvy's thin coat. "I'm sorry, laddie, but that's because you're growing up to be quite a man now. In fact, I think you are so old now that you should join the older boys today in our Bible class. Mrs. Olivier here"—he nodded toward her, and the boy's soulful gaze flitted over to her —"is going to tell you a story about another brave lad from the Bible who was also on the small side but became a king. Would you like to hear the story?"

Nodding, Darvy followed them from the room, and sensing him draw near, Colette looked down as he slipped his tiny hand into hers. Something inside cracked at his touch. *He needs me,* her heart whispered, and at the thought, her breath caught. *No one has ever needed me before.* While she longed to wrap her arms around the little fellow and kiss away his tears, all she could do was reach into her basket and pull out a cinnamon roll. "Hello there, would you like a baked goody?" she asked, bending down to his level.

For an answer, he hungrily snatched the roll from her fingers and stuffed it into his mouth, the icing smudging his pale cheeks as they entered the designated classroom.

Colette barely kept herself from gasping as she beheld the hunger in the children's faces when they locked on her basket of iced cinnamon buns. As Malcolm introduced her to each child, she handed out a roll, chastising herself for not contributing sooner as the boys crowded over, awaiting their portion. *If only I could do something more than just fill their bellies for a day.*

THE SUNSET'S glow through giant oak trees called to her, and feeling rather restless, Colette had the hired carriage drop them off five blocks from her house.

"So what did you think?" Malcolm asked, walking with her down the avenue with the Spanish moss gently waving in the branches above.

Colette ran her gloved fingertips across the black cast-iron fences with their ornate fleur-de-lis topping each rail. "You were right. They've completely stolen my heart."

Malcolm grinned. "So you'll accept the position and teach alongside me?"

"As long as you promise not to dip my curls in ink," she teased as she nodded to a lady passerby.

He stopped short, his jaw dropping.

She turned to him, a girlish laugh escaping her lips. "You honestly don't remember? You terrorized me and my poor hair ribbons in Sunday school class before they split us into a girl class and boy class."

"I could never forget," he admitted, sheepishly raking his hand through his curls as he paused by her gate. "I'm just surprised you remembered."

"I don't know how I ever forgot," she

replied before dipping into a small curtsy. "I'll begin preparing the lesson plans, but I'll see you on Wednesday evening to go over Friday's class?"

He returned a bow. "I'll be there at six o'clock sharp, and I promise not to ruin another set of your hair ribbons."

Closing the gate behind her, she knew her heart was already counting the days until she would see him again.

CHAPTER 3

"Norman Hartley is getting out of a carriage in front of your house!" Julia giggled as she poked her head through the parlor door. "You didn't tell me he was coming today, or I never would've stopped by unannounced."

Colette's head snapped up from her lesson plans to the grandfather clock. Grimacing at the time, she hurried from her writing desk to the looking glass above the mantel, smoothing her hair and pinching her cheeks.

"You should've changed out of that hideous frock," Julia lamented, stepping into the room.

"I lost track of time, and besides, the only gowns I have are in widow's colors until the seamstress can come," Colette replied as she noticed an ink stain in between her writing fingers. *Blast.* "The color isn't that repulsive, is it?"

Julia pinched the bridge of her nose and inhaled. "You would've never asked yourself this question when you were eighteen. It's not the color. It's the heavy black lace and that dowdy high collar. I wish you wouldn't wear Grandmother's old shell cameo. It's positively common. Why don't you get a carved gem cameo, one that befits your status?"

"Well, I'm not eighteen anymore. I'm a five-and-twenty-year-old widow who has forgotten how to be courted. Besides, I happen to love this piece. It reminds me of *Grandmère*." She plucked a yellow flower from the vase on her desk and tucked it into her bun. "Better?"

Julia pulled a blond curl loose from Colette's low coiffure and drew it over her shoulder. "It's the best we can manage for now, but I'm going to check with the seamstress to ensure her promptness in attending to your sad wardrobe."

"Mr. Norman Hartley to see Mrs. Olivier," the maid announced with a curtsy as Norman's confident stride sounded in the hall.

"Mrs. Olivier, you're looking quite fetching today"—he gave Colette a smile and a deep bow before turning to her sister—"and you are as pretty as ever, Miss Julia."

"Thank you, sir, and as much as I'd love to stay and visit with you, I must be on my way." She twirled out of the room before he could respond, but not before she gave her sister a conspiratorial wink.

Colette motioned for him to take a seat and signaled to the maid that she was ready for tea. "I trust your Sunday was relaxing?"

"Quite," he replied as Belinda rolled the tea cart to her mistress's side.

Colette filled his cup, worrying that they had forgotten the ease of old as the silence enveloped them. After a few minutes of stilted tête-à-tête, Colette noticed his cup sat in its saucer untouched. "Is something wrong with your tea, Mr. Hartley? Would you like me to send for another flavor? Perhaps a rooibos?"

"You found me out." He chuckled and set the cup aside. "I don't even drink tea anymore, but I didn't want to miss the chance of seeing you."

"Oh." She set her cup on the tea cart and rose. "Well, how about a turn in the garden instead? I usually go for a stroll at this time with Beignet."

"Beignet?" he asked, his brows wrinkling.

"My little dog," she explained and took his offered arm. "He's probably playing in the garden."

At the sight of the little golden dog with white markings on his face dashing about the garden in a whirlwind, Norman grinned. Beignet's antics broke the strangeness between them and they began chatting away as old friends, dropping the stiff formality of surnames as he reminisced on their mischievous childhood.

"It's nice to see you again, Colette." He tucked a loose strand behind her ear. "And now that the shipping business is growing,

I'll hopefully be seeing more of you, as I've hired a manager for my New York office. I can finally move back and set up an office here in the warehouse district."

She halted, turning to face him. "Really? How wonderful for your mother and sisters to have you home again."

"And for me to have you almost next door again."

She blushed, recollecting when Norman was the sole thought of her girlhood musings of love.

"You are different than you used to be," he murmured as they sank onto the bench under the giant magnolia tree, the gentle fragrance of its large ivory blossoms wafting down to them.

"Oh?" Her hand fluttered to the tiny crease in the corner of her eye that had come from Robert's incessant displeasure over something she had or had not done.

"You were always so carefree as a girl. What happened to that spirit of adventure that had you longing for more?"

Colette toyed with her cameo, staring past Beignet. "She was married and was widowed. Bereavement takes a toll on one's spirit."

His hand rested on her forearm. "I wouldn't have mentioned it, but Julia hinted that your marriage to Robert was not a happy one."

She pulled away and stood, wishing she could throttle Julia for divulging something she had shared in confidence. "Then why did you ask about my spirit? Did you wish to cause me pain by having me admit it?"

"I'm sorry." His face fell as he rose with his hand at her elbow. "I rather bungled what I was going to say."

Colette shied away from his touch and resumed walking.

"Please forgive me. I merely wanted to know if you still harbored dreams of adventure after your marriage with Robert or if you were content to spend the rest of your days here. . .single."

She exhaled, forcing herself to release her anger. "You're forgiven. If you must ask, now that I am nearing the end of my mourning period, I've been beginning to feel as if something is about to change." She contemplated mentioning her time with the orphans, but as it was still so new, something held her back from confiding in her old friend. She didn't want to tell him about Malcolm or her precious Bible class for fear he or society would dissuade her again.

"I've been feeling the same." At her tilted head, he raked his hands through his locks and continued, "If I wasn't such a fool as a lad, I would've realized what I was missing."

"You did what you thought best at the time, as did I."

"It has been my constant regret that I did not pursue you, Colette, and that I stood by and let you marry that man." His fists clenched. "After what Julia told me, I could've flogged myself for what my cowardice caused you to endure with a man twenty odd years your senior."

Her heart caught in her throat. *Is he confessing that he actually loved me when we were younger? That he cared for me as much as I cared for him?*

"He should've treated you like a queen," he growled. "I know I would have."

"Robert was as kind as he could be, but I

couldn't give him what he really wanted, and I think that's why he was so verbally. . ." She cleared her throat and picked up her pace a bit. *We can't do this. It was too long ago. Besides—*

He turned to her and grasped her hand in his, the warmth of his touch shooting up her arm. "All I ask for is a chance to prove to you that I don't care about your change in fortune. Give me the opportunity to woo you as I should have seven years ago. I never should've listened to my father. He wanted me to marry for wealth and so I tried to find a bride who met his expectations and my hopes for love. Yet, I never loved anyone as I knew I could've loved you if given the chance." He held her hand to his chest.

"Norman," she cautioned, her guard mounting as he stepped closer. "I'm not the same girl I once was. I've changed."

"Please," he begged, the swift beating of his heart under her hand distracting her. "I know my timing couldn't be worse, but I will make it my crusade to prove to you that money doesn't mean anything to me."

As if against her will, she found her old

hopes and dreams rising to the surface. *Is this my chance to finally be loved. . .to be wanted by a man?* Malcolm's winsome grin came to mind, and with a shake of her head, she tried to dismiss his dancing Irish eyes to focus on a man who she should actually consider, who would be accepted by her family. "I warn you it will be difficult."

"And I warn you that I never give up." He bowed and tenderly kissed her fingertips.

CHAPTER 4

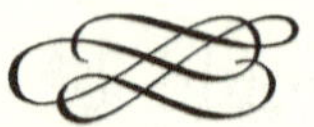

"Mrs. Olivier!" Sister Joan greeted her, surprise in her voice. "I'm not expecting you, am I?" She rubbed her hands together. "Goodness, the sisters were right. I'm getting quite forgetful in my old age."

"Oh, no! I'm sorry to come by unannounced, but"—Colette cleared her throat at her own impropriety as she clutched her storybook in one arm and her basket in the other—"I couldn't wait until Friday to see the children, so I thought I'd use a basket of fruit as an excuse to come visit." She raised her peace offering for her lack of manners.

"I hope their classes are over for the day. I wasn't sure what time they concluded, so I guessed."

The elderly woman smiled, opening the door wide for her to enter. "My dear, you never need an excuse to visit the children. I'll tell your class to meet on Darvy's floor." She winked at her. "I know he's already captured your heart as he has mine. He reminds me of Malcolm with his sweet eyes."

Malcolm certainly does have sweet ey— Colette felt her face color, but thankfully, Sister Joan had already turned toward the stairs, and within minutes, Colette was surrounded by her boys. She playfully tossed oranges to the group, happy that she'd brought more than enough for her Bible class so she could share with the younger children on Darvy's floor.

Darvy's amusement at her liveliness lit his face, but he didn't smile. He took his orange and sat in the corner, studied Colette's instruction on how to properly peel an orange, and slowly consumed his fruit as Colette opened her storybook.

Experiencing the joy of the children over an afternoon with a simple treat and a story, Colette pulled Sister Joan aside afterward and asked her assistance in putting a smile on Darvy's face.

ON FRIDAY, Colette met Malcolm on her way out the door with a giant basket of food on each arm and Belinda trailing behind with two more, grunting under the weight.

"What's all this?" Malcolm chuckled.

"Well, I noticed some of the boys seeming a bit glum," she panted, smiling all the while, "so I spoke with Sister Joan, and we thought it might be fun if I arranged to have the Bible lesson outside in Jackson Square today with a picnic lunch for the class."

"Sister Joan agreed to it?" Malcolm took the baskets from her. "Good heavens, did you bring the entire storehouse with you?"

Colette shrugged. "I wanted to be sure they'd have enough. And of course she did, as we planned it together. Do you think the boys will be surprised?"

"I think they'll be thrilled, but with fourteen boys, it'll take three carriages to carry us all to the square, as I don't trust them to take the streetcar and not get lost."

"Then it's a good thing I've arranged for my drivers to take care of that." She gestured to the row of carriages at the side of the house ready to depart.

"And then there is Mother Superior to ask," he added.

"Sister Joan has already spoken with her, and she's given us her permission and seemed quite excited for the boys' outing." She gave him a victorious smile.

"Well, then." His bright eyes met hers as excitement lit his face. "What are we waiting for?"

Her list of things to do muddled in his gaze. Shaking her head to break through the clouds, she motioned for the drivers to store Malcolm's and Belinda's loads as the butler appeared with two more baskets of dishes and blankets.

Within the hour, the rowdy group of

boys poured out of the carriages onto Jackson Square. Belinda and the butler set up the white picnic blankets and spread out the food, and Colette laid down a blanket for her and Sister Joan to sit on and keep an eye on the boys while Malcolm readied the materials for the Bible lesson.

Watching the boys play tag on the lawn, Colette smiled. "They are so content with small pleasures."

"This is likely the most fun they've had since arriving at the orphanage," Sister Joan replied. "We work hard at St. Mary's to keep the boys happy, but this is a luxury for them."

Colette chewed the inside of her cheek, thinking as the boys tumbled on the grass. "I wish they could be this happy every day."

"You can't take them on picnics all of the time," Sister Joan said, laughing, "but I know that they will cherish this day until you are as a fairy godmother in their retellings."

Heat crept up her neck. "I'm so nervous about my little part of the lesson today that I'm afraid their retellings will have more to do with how my voice shook the whole time or my dreadful execution."

Sister Joan smiled, patting her on the arm. "I'm sure you'll do fine, my dear. And if you get nervous, look to me or"—she winked—"to Malcolm."

Colette blushed in earnest as she plucked a blade of grass and proceeded to rip it into tiny pieces.

"They're too quiet by that tree," Sister Joan groaned as she stood. "I best go find out what mischief they've already managed to find."

Spotting Sister Joan, the boys waved their arms as they piped their findings of a strange insect.

Laughing at their antics, Colette leaned back on her hand, but feeling a sting, she drew it back sharply, gritting her teeth against the biting pain as she flipped over her hand to inspect it.

Malcolm's gaze flashed over and caught her pinching her palm together. "What happened?"

"It's nothing," she dismissed his concern

and attempted to pull out the splinter herself, grunting as it burrowed itself deeper.

He knelt by her side, tenderly took her hand in his rough one, and, with the greatest care, removed the splinter. Instead of releasing her, Malcolm brought her palm up to ensure he had removed all of it.

Colette felt herself drawn to him, and with him bent over her hand, she took the opportunity to study his strong jawline, which had a hint of strawberry blond stubble. With his broad shoulders so near, she couldn't help but think of what it would be like to have such a man to cherish her as his own.

He glanced up, their faces merely inches apart. "I think you'll survive," he murmured, a grin spreading over his face at catching her examining him.

"Is everything okay over here?" Sister Joan called as she crossed the green toward them.

"Thank you," she murmured and slipped her hand from his, glancing over to Belinda. "I think lunch is ready. Will you call the boys, Sister Joan?"

Helping her to her feet, Malcolm directed the charging boys over to the large blankets. The older fellows, eager for first pickings, beat out the little ones to the blankets, and after every lad was filled, Belinda presented each boy with a miniature chocolate pie with a whipped topping.

When almost every face bore evidence of the chocolate treat, Malcolm glanced up at the clock at the top of the St. Louis Cathedral. "We best begin our lesson because it's almost time to head back. Mrs. Olivier?"

Nervous to take the lead, she pasted on a smile. "Today's lesson will be short, but it's very important, so please scoot close." Colette patted the blanket beside her and motioned for the boys to crowd together. Darvy snuggled up next to her, and she couldn't help but look to Malcolm and smile.

"We're going to talk about John 6:35 where our Lord Jesus Christ tells us, 'I am the bread of life: he that cometh to me shall never hunger; and he that believeth on me shall never thirst.' Today, we gave you cake and milk and filled your bellies, but as you know, boys will get very hungry again by nightfall. Jesus is talking about food for your soul"—she tapped Darvy's chest near his heart. "For a long time, I felt alone, and I searched for a way to fill the hole in my heart because I was hungry for something more. I tried to fill the void being the very best girl I could manage, which as you know can be difficult when others tempt you to retaliate when teased."

At this the boys poked each other, and Malcolm had to intervene to turn the attention back to Colette.

Clearing her throat, Colette continued, "But being good wasn't enough to make the hole go away. I needed something more, *Someone* more." She glanced at Malcolm, who gave her an encouraging nod. "Do you want to know how I stopped feeling hungry and alone and how you can, too?"

Some of the boys seemed a little restless, but her gaze locked on the young Italian boy, Luca, whose eyes were bright with thirst. *Please, Lord, let me get through to them.* "If you believe in Jesus as your Savior and pray for Him to enter your heart, you will never again feel hunger in your soul, for He will fill that void inside." She pressed her hand to her chest as her voice wavered.

Malcolm reached over and gently squeezed her hand. "Thank you, Mrs. Olivier. Let's bow our heads." With a brief prayer, Malcolm dismissed the boys, and as they dashed away for one last romp, she overheard Luca asking Malcolm for a moment alone later.

"See? It wasn't so bad," the old nun whispered with a smile, her wrinkles creating a halo over her brow. She clapped her hands and herded the boys back into the carriages.

As Colette bid each boy farewell at the orphanage, her heart filled at their overwhelming gratitude. Ruffling Darvy's hair, she thought, *If only I could bring all these boys home with me.* She turned in the doorway, relishing Darvy's laughter as Malcolm gave his animated interpretation of the day's events to Mother Superior. *It's not as if I don't have the space, time, or funds.* She chewed the inside of her lip and turned away.

It was almost dinnertime when Colette arrived home, and stripping off her gloves, she sighed with exhaustion as she spied a gentleman's small calling card on the silver tray in the hallway with its top left corner folded. Flipping it over, she found Norman's name with a request for dinner in his fancy script and felt a twinge of guilt that she hadn't even thought of him all day.

CHAPTER 5

Norman held the gilded back of her chair as she slipped into her seat in the lavish hunter-green room with gold trim. *Antoine's* ornate golden chandelier lent a delicate glow that caught the crystal glasses on the tables, making the walls sparkle.

Taking his place across from her, Norman lifted his glass and ceremoniously clinked it against hers. "I believe this is the first time we've ever dined together in public without a family member or your old nurse as a chaperone."

"I think I can take care of myself." Colette winked at him, lifted her menu, and located her favorite creole appetizer, *chair de crabes au gratin*.

"You most certainly can." He reached across the table and clasped her hand. "You look breathtaking."

Her mouth watered a bit at the thought of the breaded crab dish. "I'm sorry, did you say something?"

He chuckled and released her hand. "Well, that hasn't changed." At her raised brow, he expounded, "Until you get food, you can't carry on much of a conversation."

She grimaced and set aside the menu. "I'm sorry. It's been far too long since I last came here with Robert."

"Ah, yes." He shifted in his seat, uncomfortable with any mention of Robert.

"I do have a bit of news that I'd like to share with you." She smoothed her amethyst silk skirt before draping the fine linen napkin over her lap. "I'm helping with the Bible class at the boys' orphanage, St. Mary's, and—"

"Really?" His glass chinked rather loudly

as he hit the rim of his plate in setting it down.

"Well, yes," she stumbled in her haste to explain, "I wanted to volunteer at the church, as I used to do it all the time, but shamefully, I haven't for years because, um —" She paused, not knowing how to politely phrase, *Since I was married and Robert forbade me from it.* "Well, let's just say that things didn't work out. After visiting the orphanage, I found myself wishing there was more that I could do as the orphanage is so crowded and the children almost never get a chance to play off grounds, so I brought the lads on a picnic yesterday."

"How kind of you." Norman gave her an almost patronizing grin.

"Thank you," she pressed onward, ignoring her agitation, "but I wanted to discuss something with you. After the picnic, I began thinking—"

"Sorry I'm late," Julia panted as she joined them. "I couldn't decide on which dress to wear as a chaperone. I figured my emerald-green dress was as austere as I could manage."

"Miss Julia!" Norman dropped his napkin from his lap in his haste to rise and bow, but as she was already seated, he managed a half bow.

"I may be a widow who can take care of herself, but I haven't forgotten the proper etiquette for dining with a gentleman." She leaned toward him and whispered dramatically, "You don't think I want the socialites to catch wind of secret rendezvous with a mysterious suitor, do you?"

"Funny." Norman smirked.

"Have you ordered yet?" Julia motioned for the waiter to fill her glass.

"I was waiting for you." Colette handed her menu to Julia as her stomach growled. "Please tell me that you already know what you want." She pressed her hand to her corset, praying her stomach would mind its manners.

"Of course. Now, you two pretend that I'm not here." Julia rattled off her order to the waiter before he turned to take Norman's and Colette's.

Taking Julia at her word, Norman returned to the topic at hand. "So, you brought these boys out to Jackson Square on your own?"

"Oh, no." She inwardly cringed at the thought of wrangling all the boys by herself. "I teach with a gentleman named Malcolm Reilly. He makes certain the boys stay in line."

"Reilly? Never heard of an Irish *gentleman* by that name. Is it proper to teach alongside him?" He motioned at Julia, his nose pinching. "I mean, you've known me your whole life, yet you teach with this man alone."

"Sister Joan is usually present for their lessons." *But not all the time.* She thought of Malcolm's hand caressing her palm and realized Norman might be right to question her. "It's not as if he were taking me to dinner," she reassured him as much as herself. "Besides, it was the pastor's wife, his mother, who enlisted my help, and as the nuns adore him, I feel that is as good a character recommendation as one could get."

"Oh, the nuns approve of him? Sounds

like quite the catch," he mumbled sarcastically as he buttered his sweet potato roll.

"Anyway, to continue my story, when I saw how happy the children were outside of the orphanage, I began thinking that I have so much room in my mansion, it's really a shame to keep it all to myself."

Norman choked on his drink and Julia pressed her napkin to her mouth, a snort escaping. She waved them onward. "Sorry, sorry! I'm not here. Keep talking."

"You can hardly have them in your home," Norman replied with a slow smile.

"And why not?" she retorted, disappointed at the mockery her dreams were receiving.

"Really, Colette. Mr. Hartley will begin to think you're serious," Julia interrupted, forgetting her silent role as she dabbed away her tears of amusement.

"But I am serious. I have more than enough room, while they barely have a place to lay their heads or enough food to go around. The caretaker said that they scarcely have less than four hundred children at a time."

"It's not as if you can fit that many in your home, either," Norman muttered.

"No, but I can fit at least twenty boys, and if I finish out the half story, I can fit another six boys," she continued, her heart pounding as she confided her dream of a school for the first time.

"Twenty-six? Why would you want so many to fill your mansion when an orphanage could get the job done more efficiently if you *donated* your funds? I know a few of the men on the board at St. Mary's, and I'm sure they'd appreciate your sizable donation."

"Sister Joan sparked an idea that has been brewing in my head for the last twenty-four hours. I could transform my mansion into a legitimate school and teach the boys a trade, provide cotillion classes, and raise their stations in life through education." Her eyes glistened with excitement. "While I may not be able to help *all* the boys at once. I can change the lives of dozens and then, over time, hundreds."

"That's my sister. Always so generous at heart that she fails to see the logic in the moment." Julia patted her on the arm. "You've never been a mother, and heaven knows, with only a sister, you've never experienced rearing boys. It was a very sweet thought, my sister, but surely you can understand why we can't take you seriously?"

Colette opened her mouth to protest, but Julia gave her a little kick under the table, pursed her lips, and sent her a pointed stare as the waiter set their plates before them. Colette clenched her jaw and stared at her appetizer. Since Robert's death, she hadn't thought anyone would try to control her desire to serve again. . .much less her sister or Norman Hartley.

OVER THE NEXT FEW WEEKS, Colette did not bring up the school to Norman again. Instead, she prayed and planned over her school in the quiet of her home until she was certain it was not in fact, as Norman suggested, a passing fancy. When she was certain of the Lord's hand, she hired an architect to draw up the plans to convert her home, and upon delivery of his work, she tucked the plans into a portfolio and left for Malcolm's office.

"Mrs. Olivier"—concern lit the green flecks in Malcolm's eyes as he rose from his desk—"is everything okay? I thought we weren't meeting until tomorrow afternoon."

"Oh, yes, but I had something that couldn't wait." The high collar of her dress stuck to her throat from the heavy morning humidity. "I know I've only been helping you for a short time, but I'd like to ask you something."

He motioned for her to have a seat, giving his full attention.

"I was praying about what else I could do for the boys at the orphanage, more than teaching classes and the occasional picnic."

His brows shot up. "Oh?"

She laid her portfolio on his desk. "I've been thinking that I'd like to turn my home into a school for boys where they can learn a trade and have a foster mother along with a houseful of brothers."

He blew out his cheeks. "Colette, er,

Mrs. Olivier," he corrected his slip, "I don't know what to say."

"I know you studied at Miss Wright's night school, so I'd like to offer you a job as one of the teachers and my counterpart." She cleared her throat. "I know, it's a strange position I'm proposing, but I could think of no one I'd rather have as my partner in the day-to-day operations of the school."

His jaw slacked as he crossed his arms and leaned against his cane-back chair, exhaling.

"I hope I haven't offended you." She dipped her head. "I—I know you work hard at your office here, but I remembered how you said you wished to teach, and I was hoping you could put to use what Miss Wright taught you and guide me in operating a school for boys."

"I'm not offended at all." Malcolm laughed, running his hand through his hair. "I'm simply speechless."

Colette let out her pent-up breath. *Thank goodness.*

He rested his hand on her arm before

thinking better of it and pulled away. "You're sure about this? Because once the school is open, it'll be hard to turn back without upsetting the lives of a lot of boys."

"I've prayed extensively about this, and I believe that it's what I'm to do for the rest of my days. I had been wondering how I could use Robert's fortune, and this is the obvious route."

"You know that no one in your family will approve"—he drummed his fingers on the desk—"and I'm sure your friends won't look kindly on your decision, either."

Friends, meaning Norman? "No, but I'm done bending to their opinions. I must listen to the Lord. I've ignored Him in the past, but I won't again."

He took her hand in his; the roughness of his skin seemed to peel away the layers of protection she had spent years forming. "Then, Mrs. Olivier, you mustn't let anything stand in your way."

"Would you like to see what I have in mind?" She grinned, happy to share her news, as she rose and opened her portfolio.

"Absolutely." He stood and leaned on the desk to peer over her prints.

Taking him through the plans, floor by floor, Colette explained how the first floor would be for classrooms, the second floor's west wing for the youngest children and the teacher, the third floor for the middle grades, and the half story for the oldest boys.

"So what do you think?" she finished, breathlessly.

"Quite the undertaking for just the two of us." He rubbed the base of his neck.

"Yes, but with your help and with another teacher, we can manage." She slowly turned to the sketch of the garden house, her heart racing. "I thought that for propriety's sake, it would be best to have the old gardener's house turned into a comfortable home for you, offering you privacy, but, uh. . .that is"—she paused, biting her lip in the fashion Robert had hated—"if you even *want* the job." She turned to him, the seriousness of her question weighing her shoulders: "Will you be my partner in raising these boys?"

He stuck out his hand. "I'm your man."

At those words, she slipped her hand into his, and her heart stirred as it hadn't in years. *Yes, you just might be my man.* She took a deep breath, reminded herself of Norman, and banished the thought. "Wonderful. The interviews for the teaching position begin tomorrow morning at nine o'clock sharp."

CHAPTER 6

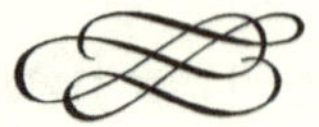

Colette groaned into her hands. "How is everyone we've interviewed so far so ill suited for teaching boys?"

"Let's hope this next person will be conducive, because she's the last candidate." Malcolm leaned back on the two legs of his chair.

A pretty girl with dark locks poked her head into the doorway. "Good morning, I'm—"

Malcolm's chair legs slammed onto the hardwood. "Katie?"

"Malcolm Reilly?" She gasped as he stood and extended his hand.

"I thought your name sounded familiar. Patrick's little sister all grown up. So good to see you! The last time I saw you was when you were in pigtails."

She laughed. "It's been quite a long time, and as you can see from my references, I go by Katherine now." She turned her attention to Colette and curtsied. "Mrs. Olivier, thank you so much for agreeing to see me."

Colette nodded and gestured for her to have a seat. "We were eager to meet you, Miss O'Dell, but as you and Mr. Reilly have already met, why don't you tell me a little bit about yourself?"

Miss O'Dell bubbled with enthusiasm, describing her studies and how even though she lacked experience in the classroom, she was more than ready to take on the challenge of teaching a class of rowdy boys from her experience of growing up in a houseful of brothers.

At the end of the interview, Colette knew Miss O'Dell was the one for the job even though she was slightly annoyed by how much Malcolm seemed to enjoy the young lady's giddiness.

When Malcolm returned from taking rather a long time to show Katherine to the door, he reclaimed his seat, swiveling to face Colette. "Well, that was a pleasant surprise. She's studied at a fine school, and while this will be her first teaching position, I think she'll be a great fit." He brushed off his hands as if his job were done.

"You're certain the boys would respond well to someone so. . .young?" she ventured, testing to see if he thought she was indeed as pretty as her imagination led her to believe.

He grinned. "It may actually work in her favor, as they are more likely to behave for such a bonny face."

Bonny face? She fought back a grimace, trying not to dislike the girl before she even started working. Colette stretched her back. "Well, we know for sure that the first five candidates will not be a suitable match for our school."

"And your thoughts on Miss O'Dell? Is there anything holding you back from hiring her?" Malcolm's brow creased.

Besides the fact that she's gorgeous? "Her

age," she settled, leaving out her youthful glow and bright blue eyes devoid of crow's feet.

"The boys will be respectful. I'll see to it," he assured her in a shielding tone, causing her heart to twitch.

Upset by her own jealously of Malcolm's protectiveness toward the pretty teacher, she examined her hesitation. "Well, in that case, let's hire Miss O'Dell."

He grinned, scraping back his chair as he stood. "I'll go to her house at once and tell her the good news myself, and we can get started on ordering some supplies tomorrow morning."

"Marvelous." Colette returned his smile, praying her heart would catch up with her head.

AS THEY WALKED about the parlor, Colette jotted down instructions on her notepad for the removal of the Persian rug and the antiquities, how many desks they needed, and the possible placement of the teacher's desk.

"And speaking of the teacher's desk," Malcolm interjected, "have you given mind where the new schoolmarm will stay?"

"I was planning on giving her the largest west-wing room and having a sort of sitting area set up in the corner of her room. Do you think that will be to her liking? Or will she expect two rooms?"

"Miss O'Dell isn't picky." He pointed at a spot between the front windows. "I think she'd like to have the morning light on her papers, so let's place the desk there."

"You know her well enough to know that?" She bit back a snort and again questioned her animosity toward Miss O'Dell. *She's been nothing but sweet to you, so behave.*

"When I stopped by her parents' house last night, they invited me to stay for dinner and I learned a little bit more about her," he replied, seeming not to suspect her reaction.

"That's nice," she murmured, thinking that it was quite the opposite of nice, and turned her attention back to the schoolroom and away from this troubling turn of events. "So, what do you think about adding bookshelv—"

"So it's true. You really are turning your home into a school," Norman stated from the doorway, gripping the brim of his hat. "I didn't think I'd be hearing such life-altering news from Julia."

Colette crossed the room, rested her hand on his arm, and lowered her voice to keep Malcolm from overhearing. "I hadn't planned on announcing it yet. The school won't be ready until mid-August."

"Then don't. It's absurd to devote the best years of your life to a houseful of children," he growled, his brows knitting together.

"You forget that you were the one who encouraged me." Colette gave him a wink to smooth his temper as she threaded her arm through his and led him out to the garden, hoping the fresh air would cool his temper.

He frowned as he flung open the garden gate, stepping onto the public sidewalk.

"You're angry with me, aren't you?"

He looked down at her, the darkness in his features fading as he cupped her cheek. "I'm merely concerned and a bit hurt you didn't feel the need to confide in me of your plans and that I had to find out about this from your sister."

She inclined her head, understanding his point of view. "I'm sorry. I should've told you in person, but when I tried to tell you at the dinner, you dismissed it."

"I didn't know you were so serious about it." His voice strained, and clearing his throat, he tugged on his hat. "I suppose you still need an hour before the dinner party to dress, so I'll take a walk."

"Won't you wait for me in the parlor? I lost track of time, but I can be ready in a half hour." She attempted to stay him.

"I could use the walk to calm down. I won't be much of a dinner partner if I'm sullen." He dug his fists into his pockets and trudged down St. Charles Avenue. "I'll see you in a bit, Colette."

HER FAMILY DID NOT TAKE the news well. After an awkward dinner of her parents trying to convince her to fulfill her calling in a less expensive way, she flung her skirts behind her as she stepped down from the carriage onto her drive, ignoring Norman's offered hand.

"Colette." He grasped her by the elbow, stopping her. "Please don't be angry with me. I was taken aback by your determination to open this school. I had thought that you were taking time to recover after your mourning period, but now that you're spending most of your fortune on this place, I think it's time I step in with some advice."

"You already tried that at dinner and it didn't quite work out for you." *So you best bide your tongue,* she finished in her head.

"Yes, and I wish to apologize for my overbearing tone earlier," he replied, drawing her hand in his.

"Oh?" The tension in her shoulders lessened a fraction.

"However, I do believe in the message I was attempting to convey," he finished.

Unbelievable. She dropped her hand from his grasp and marched toward the garden, fearing what she might say in her anger. "I don't need your approval." She shoved open the iron garden gate. "Honestly, Norman, I thought you would be more supportive, especially after you defended me at dinner tonight."

"Your father's friends had no business offering their opinion, but as we are courting, I believe I can be concerned!"

She clenched her jaw, swallowed back her retort, and barely resisted slamming the gate between them. "You are crossing the line."

"Crossing a line? I thought we were more than casual acquaintances. Doesn't that give me a right to an opinion?"

Her cheeks flushed. "An opinion, yes, but authority, no. Until all of this settles down, I think we need to take some time to reevaluate our relationship."

He inhaled deeply as he halted her promenade, grabbing her hand and gently pulling her toward him. "Colette."

Norman gave her the smile that she knew melted girls' hearts everywhere, except tonight. It wouldn't work. She looked down to avoid his hypnotic stare and keep her thoughts clear. "No. I won't discuss this with you any further tonight."

"I think, my dear Colette, that we are just too different."

Her startled gaze met his. "What?"

"We want different things. Even though it's your spirit that has always drawn me to you, I'm too traditional for you, my dear girl." Norman stroked her cheek with his thumb. "I want to be with you, but not enough to share you with a houseful of boys that are not ours."

Colette's shoulders caved as the wind left her lungs. *Surely he isn't leaving me a second time?* "Are you certain?"

He lifted her chin and tenderly kissed her cheek. "I'm sorry, but I think we are better off as friends, and if you really think about it, you know I'm right."

The doubts she had not wanted to admit having rose, and instead of being crushed once more, she knew he was right. "I'm sorry." She reached up to brush a curl from his forehead. "I'm sorry I could not be the girl you left behind."

With a tender smile, she slipped inside to find Malcolm packing away the last of the parlor's antiques in an open crate. "Oh, you didn't have to do this. I was going to finish up tonight," she said, setting down her reticule on the settee and stiffly peeling off her gloves, still in shock over Norman.

"I don't mind," he replied, tucking a figurine in the straw. "How was dinner?"

She laughed without mirth. "Well, between Norman and Julia, the news was released prematurely. One would have thought that I was committing a felony with the way everyone responded." She removed the last vase from the fireplace mantel and handed it to Malcolm.

"Well, I'm sure they did think of it as a crime," Malcolm replied as he hefted the crate into his arms.

"What on earth do you mean?" she asked, following him up the stairs to the east wing.

"They raised you to marry into a fortune, and now that you have access to do what you will with it, you are doing the very opposite of what they intended," he surmised, setting down the crate outside her door.

"The opposite being?"

"Spending it on the family or using it to raise your station in a way that would still support them. You have to be strong in your decision. The school opens in two weeks, so now is the time to back out if you need to."

"No, absolutely not. I've tried their way before and I was miserable." She leaned against her door and looked up to him. "Do you think I've taken leave of my senses? That I'm letting my feelings carry me away?"

He took her hands in his, and with kindness in his voice, he whispered, "I think what you are doing is a mighty fine thing. You're going to change the lives of hundreds."

At his words, she found herself flooded with strength. She thought of Norman's aversion to her calling and of Malcolm's opposite reaction. *Is this what love is meant to be like? If only I'd had Robert's support, how different my life would've been.*

CHAPTER 7

With the rooms complete and the last chalk tablet set on the school desk, Colette was eager to open the school and welcome her boys.

At the sound of carriage wheels crunching the gravel drive, Malcolm peeked behind the schoolroom's lace curtain. "Katie, I mean, Miss O'Dell is here!"

Colette checked her watch pin. "We have just under an hour until the boys arrive, so would you mind walking about to ensure all is prepared while I get her settled into her bedroom?" She smoothed the front of her new navy gown and straightened her cameo, which was fastened to a ruffled lace jabot.

"Certainly." The front door opened, and Colette watched his face grow bright at Katherine's presence. "Miss O'Dell, welcome home."

The pretty teacher untied her cloak and dropped into a small curtsy. "Mr. Reilly and Mrs. Olivier, I must tell you it's *such* an honor to be working as one of your first teachers," she babbled, her hands fluttering in the air. "Who would've thought that *I* would be appointed as head schoolmarm on my first job?"

Colette smiled at the girl's enthusiasm. "We're honored to have you, and while the duties of the head teacher shall rest mainly with you, Mr. Reilly and I will be here to help ease your burden with his classes and mine."

"It's wonderfully clever to teach such a useful class as Mr. Reilly's trade workshop," Katherine replied as the underbutlers appeared with her rather worn trunk between them.

"I hope the boys will only ever learn

things here that are useful," Colette replied quietly. "As a debutante, I was taught all manner of impractical things."

The young girl blushed, abruptly aware of her faux pas.

"If you'll follow me, I'll show you to your room." Colette smiled to put her at ease, gesturing her toward the stairs.

In the hall, Katherine complimented the ornate wallpaper, and when Colette swung open the west-wing bedroom door, the new teacher gasped.

Colette paused, trying to read her expression. "Is it not to your liking? I wish I could've given you two rooms for a bedroom and parlor set, but I needed the other room for the boys, and I thought a breakfast nook in the corner would suffice—"

Katherine pressed a hand to her mouth. "It's beautiful. I've never had a bedroom to myself before, and I never imagined living in one half as grand."

Colette cleared her throat. "Well, um, I'm very glad it pleases you. Shall I send one of the maids to help you unpack?"

"Maids?" She giggled, stroking the heavy

curtains as she passed. "It wouldn't be worth the time for them to climb the stairs for I only have a trunk of dresses, as the other trunk is full of books and school things that I thought might prove helpful." She knelt down and pried open the lid with a grunt. "It gets a little stuck sometimes." She gave a nervous giggle and shook out a serviceable gown of navy and spread it out on the bed, followed by a brown frock and a gray.

Pleased that Katherine had such sensible gowns to keep the distractions at a minimum, she nodded with approval. "Well, I'll leave you to get settled, and then I'll give you the tour with the boys? They should be arriving any minute."

"Oh? I'll come with you, then," she said, tossing a stocking back into the trunk. "I don't want to miss the grand opening of Mrs. Olivier's School for Boys."

Colette warmed to her enthusiasm and knew they could become friends if only. . .she paused with her hand on the mahogany stair rail. *Am I jealous?* She attempted to dismiss the ridiculous notion. *I've nothing to be jealous of. Malcolm has no commitment to me other than being my employee and is free to see whomever he likes.* To her chagrin, her rebellious heart clenched at the thought of Malcolm and Katherine together, and she wished that society's rules weren't quite so limiting. She bit her lip. Thinking how her parents had reacted to the news of the school, she could just imagine how they would respond if she acted on her growing feelings for Malcolm.

"They're on St. Charles Avenue, Mrs. Olivier," one of the maids called up to her, breaking her reverie. "The underbutler was on the lookout for them."

Hastening down the stairs and out the front door, she found Malcolm already on the bottom step. "I can't believe our first set of boys are here." Colette clasped her hands in front of her satin skirt as she waited for the two carriages to pull into the driveway with two boys from each grade from first to sixth.

"There's no turning back now." Malcolm smiled down at her.

"I would never want to," she returned. *Give it a week and I'm sure you will think dif-*

ferently, she could almost hear her mother say if she were present.

"When will the rest be arriving?" Katherine asked.

"I checked with St. Mary's, and they said they'll be sending the additional fourteen boys from the seventh to twelfth grades this afternoon. We wanted to have time to settle the younger group," Malcolm explained to her.

Spotting the carriage, Colette barely contained a squeal as she grasped Malcolm's rough hand. He looked down at her, surprise lighting his eyes. Colette dropped his hand, her face flushing, and turned her attention to the halted carriage.

Darvy leaned out of the window and yelled and waved both his arms in the air. "Mrs. Olivier! Mrs. Olivier!" The small dark-haired boy hopped down from the carriage, skipping a step, and ran straight into her arms as they both giggled and began chattering away.

Kissing his cheek before releasing him, Colette focused on the other eleven lads and Sister Joan, who had agreed to chaperone the boys until they reached her care. "Hello, I'm Mrs. Olivier, and I want to welcome you to Mrs. Olivier's School for Boys, your new home and your new family. Let's get you established in your rooms, and when you hear the gong, meet us at the foot of the stairs for the tour of the grounds."

The boys cautiously climbed the stairs to the second and third floors, some with distrust in their expressions and others with fear as Colette showed the boys to their assigned rooms. Keeping the six youngest boys on the second floor in case they grew afraid at night, she directed the rest of the boys to the third floor, saving the large half story for the eldest lads.

After fifteen minutes of orderly chaos as each boy settled into his bed, Colette had Belinda sound the gong, bringing the boys tumbling down the stairs and sending Beignet into a bouncing barking fit at the invaders of his house. The boys snickered at the little dog's hysterics with Darvy imitating the sound, much to the maids' annoyance as they pressed their hands to their ears.

Colette overheard Katherine giggle from behind and whisper to Malcolm, "They're going to have to get used to the noise, or I'm afraid Mrs. Olivier might find herself in need of replacements within the week."

"Let's pray that isn't the case, else you and I will have our hands full," Malcolm returned, teasing in his voice.

Raising her hands, she called for the boys' attention, and as they already knew Malcolm, she introduced them to Katherine, who gave them a brilliant smile and curtsy. Colette thanked her with a small nod. "Now, I know that some of you"—she looked the twin third-graders who had lost their final parent to illness—"have suffered a great loss recently and others, in the distant past. I may understand a little of what you're going through as my own husband died two years ago, leaving me quite alone in this house. It was my greatest wish to have a child, but as you see"—she gestured to her empty arms with a little laugh—"I didn't until this day. I want you all to think of me as your mother, or if you can't, maybe at least your favorite auntie who loves you all more than she can express. My door is always open to you."

As if shy by her warmth, the boys shuffled their feet at the end of her speech, but Darvy sidled up next to her, slipping his hand in hers.

"Well, enough of that. Let's explore, shall we?" She released Darvy's hand with a gentle squeeze and brought the group of twelve boys through to the classrooms, tailed by Malcolm and Katherine, who she noticed kept their heads inclined toward one another, whispering to each other.

Sister Joan came up to her elbow, shaking her head as she chuckled. "With all that sweet talk, these boys are going to attempt to run right over you"—she nodded to Darvy—"especially that one. He's already got you wrapped around his finger."

Colette's face warmed as she scooped up the still yapping dog in an attempt to quiet him. "Did I sound foolish?"

Sister Joan rubbed the top of Beignet's head, her gold wedding band catching in the light. "You sounded genuine, my dear. However, be prepared to love them with not only gentleness but firmness." She laughed at Colette's tilted head. "In other words, don't let them get away with murder. You won't be doing them any favors when they leave here." She nodded toward the group. "You better give the tour. I fear they're getting restless."

Colette clapped her hands and led the group through the classrooms, listing off which classes would be taught by which teacher. Seeing the boys' noses wrinkle at the mention of her cotillion classes and hearing disgruntled mumbles about frilly lessons, she bit back a snicker as Beignet wriggled in her arms. "And beyond the dining room, the doors lead out into the gardens," Colette called, setting down the dog and swinging open the french doors.

The boys hooted as they flooded outside behind the dog and ran over the manicured lawn, rolling in the grass and climbing the large oak and magnolia trees. One of the boys picked up a fallen bunch of Spanish moss and draped the gray filth over his head to form a beard.

"Tommy! You want to give the school

lice on the first day?" Malcolm shouted and scrambled over to him, swiping it off his head.

Colette cringed, remembering Mother's prediction that the boys would cause the place to swarm with insects, ruining her costly Parisian furniture.

"Mrs. Olivier?" Belinda called from the veranda, panting from her haste. "The last of the carriages are pulling into the drive with the older boys! They're two hours early! What are we going to do?"

Letting Malcolm and Katherine deal with the lice-infested moss for the moment, Colette gathered her skirts and hurried toward the front of the house with Sister Joan and the maid following closely behind. "We're going to take it one day at a time."

COLETTE TOSSED and turned until she knew slumber was not going to visit her unless she had some chamomile. Pushing aside the mosquito netting, Colette slipped on a loose ivory blouse and stepped into her pink skirt but left her hair spilling down over her shoulders. Grabbing her blue silk shawl embroidered with bright flowers, she tiptoed down to the kitchen in her bare feet to brew some tea.

With the kettle on to boil, she rested her head in her hands on the rustic kitchen table and began to pray for each and every boy, beginning with the youngest. She paused in her petitions when she came to the names of the seventh-graders. *Good heavens. What are their names?* Feeling like quite the terrible mother for forgetting their names, she jumped up to fetch her ledger, when she heard a scratching at the side door of the kitchen.

Knowing all the children were in bed, she gripped her teacup, ready to fight should a robber endanger her children. The lock popped and the door clicked open. With a frightful yell, she hurled her tea and the hot contents into the face of the intruder. The robber ducked, avoiding the cup as it shattered into the wall, steeping him.

"What on earth?" Malcolm wiped off his shirtsleeves.

Her shoulders caved as she pressed a hand to her pounding heart and leaned on the table. "I thought you were a burglar!"

"And you were going to fight him off with a cup of hot tea?" He chuckled, swiping a rag from the counter. "Good thing you have me to watch out for you."

"What are you doing prowling about at this time of night?" She crossed her arms over her chest, aware of her hair flowing down to her waist.

He paused before answering, his gaze lingering on her golden curls before he looked down, rubbing his hands on the rag. "I was hungry and I left my key inside, so I used my lock kit." He lifted a small, rolled-up leather pouch.

"Why do you have a loc—"

"My grandfather was a locksmith. I don't remember him too well, but it was the only thing I had when I was brought to the orphanage, so I learned how to use it."

"I bet you gave the nuns a frightful time with that little toy." She giggled. A sudden weakness from the fright of Malcolm's unexpected appearance gripped her and she sank down onto the kitchen chair, clutching her silk shawl to her neck.

"I had it taken away more than once." He grinned. "Well, I'll leave you to your tea and come back later."

"Would you like some chamomile tea? I made a fresh pot, and it would be a shame to only share it with the wall when you could use some to help you sleep." Warning bells sounded, but she ignored them. "And I spied some leftover cinnamon rolls under the glass dome, over there." She pointed to the corner of the kitchen.

"Chamomile would be nice," he admitted as he retrieved the sweet roll and another teacup, taking a seat as Colette poured him a cup. "Don't know why I'm so awake. Must've been all the excitement of the day."

"Me, too," she agreed, lifting her cup in a salute. "Day one is over, but our journey is just beginning."

"Here, here." He clinked his cup against hers. His gaze caught Colette's, and it seemed as if he was trying to find the right words when one of the maids appeared in the threshold.

"Oh! Excuse me, Mrs. Olivier," she gasped, clutching her robe, no doubt shocked at seeing her mistress with her hair down and alone with Malcolm.

With flaming cheeks, Colette grabbed her teacup and saucer, made her excuses to them both, and vanished upstairs, reminding herself that she had done nothing wrong.

CHAPTER 8

"And, one-two-three-four and one-two-three-fou—" She gritted her teeth as Tommy's foot slammed onto her toes.

"Sorry, Mrs. Olivier," he mumbled, stepping away to let her catch her breath as she limped it off to keep from crying out.

Six weeks of dance lessons and he still can't manage the simple step. She smoothed the front of her canary-yellow dress to compose herself. With its lace cuffs and ruffles, she knew her dress was a bit ostentatious for a dance lesson, but she tried to convince herself the color was for her own sake and not because Malcolm was about the house and she wanted to look her best. "It's quite all right, Tommy. You need to practice, though, to be ready for the cotillion dance in three weeks if you want to impress the girls' Sunday school class."

A chuckle came from the parlor's doorway, and she spied Malcolm attempting to wipe the grin from his face. "Mr. Reilly," she almost sighed with relief, "I think it might help the class"—she gestured to the older students that she was endeavoring to prepare for being released into society—"if you demonstrated." She lifted her hands into position, waiting for him to step into her arms.

Malcolm shrugged. "Tommy seems to be doing well enough."

"Yes, but"—she waved him over, with her right hand still in position—"it will help them to see it executed without flaws."

He averted his gaze. "I'm sorry. I can't."

She dropped her hands and turned back to Tommy, her pride smarting. "Well, then. Since Mr. Reilly isn't available, let's try this again, shall we?" She instructed Luca to play the pianoforte, starting the piece from the middle.

"Mind if I cut in?" Norman asked, stepping over the rolled-up carpet to claim her.

"Mr. Hartley!" She gasped as his arm wrapped around her waist and he whirled her around in the waltz, saving her poor feet from further injury. "You know just when to rescue a girl, don't you?"

"Your poor, dainty toes." He looked down at her feet, spotting the black boot marks on the tips of her dancing slippers. He captured her eyes with his somber ones. "Can you ever forgive me? I'm a wretched oaf. I was so focused on my bullheaded, so-called logic that I didn't even consider your calling to raise these boys," Norman whispered into her ear. "Give me another chance, my darling. Say yes, and I'll never give you cause to doubt me again. To begin, allow me to take you to dinner tonight?"

Seeing now that Malcolm had no interest in her, she intended not to make a further fool of herself. *Why should I pass my chance of love in the hopes Malcolm will eventually want me?* "You know I never could stay angry with you for very long." She lifted her voice and her smile to the class, "See, lads, how Mr. Hartley guides me about the room? His grip is confident, yet gentle."

"Dancing is all about making the lady shine," Norman added, mischief tainting his voice. "You're merely an instrument to display her beauty, making you the object of envy of every man in the room."

Colette rolled her eyes as the boys cackled at his instruction. "Really, Norman," she whispered. "Such ideas you will give them."

"It's true, though. With you in my arms, I am the envy of every man."

Blushing, she turned her focus back to the boys, catching Malcolm sauntering off behind them with his hands shoved in his pockets.

STANDING in front of the class, Colette rubbed her sweaty palms discreetly on her yellow skirt. "I suppose you are all wondering why I am here. Miss O'Dell just received word that her father has taken ill, so I gave her the next few days off. Mr. Reilly is currently working on unclogging the plumbing"—the boys chortled and pointed to Tommy, but she ignored them, continuing—"so I'm taking over her class."

She directed everyone to take out their arithmetic books. *Lord, help me. I haven't looked at a mathematics problem since I was a girl.* The rain plinked against the wavy glass panes as she cracked open Katie's teacher's guide and cringed. As a socialite out for a rich husband, arithmetic had been grossly neglected at her finishing school. The only math she had needed to know was how to count how many girls she was competing against for which eligible bachelors.

After an hour of trying to teach twelve grades of arithmetic to a class of fidgeting boys, she felt as if her head might explode. A golden ray fell onto her page, and glancing up, she realized it had stopped raining. *Thank God.* "Let's take a quick recess while there's a break in the rain." The classroom erupted, and sinking back into her chair, she rubbed her temples. *How does Katherine do this? It's excruciating.*

Pulling the bell cord for some much-deserved tea, she heard footsteps on the stairs. She pinched her cheeks and drew her curl over her shoulder before she reached for the nearest book, wishing to appear as collected as Miss O'Dell. Feeling slightly silly but not enough to drop her carefree charade, she turned the page without reading it.

Hearing shouts from outside, she rustled to the french doors and peeked through the lace curtains to see the twins in an all-out brawl. "Joshua and Jordan! Stop that at once!" she cried as she dropped her book and dashed down the veranda steps. The boys ignored her and fell to the ground, grappling in the soggy grass, turning it into a mud pit.

Gritting her teeth against the mess, she attempted to wrench the two apart, but a misplaced punch knocked her off her feet and face-first into the mud. Colette gasped as she raised herself onto her elbows, feeling the cold mud seep through to her skin.

The horrified twins halted their fight as a pair of strong hands assisted her to her feet. "We're so sorry, Mrs. Olivier," they cried, attempting to wipe off her gown while she scraped the mud from her face, groaning as her cheek was already growing tender.

Malcolm gripped her shoulders, and turning her to inspect her face, he grimaced. "You're going to have quite the shiner."

Colette tried to tip her chin out of his hand. *At least the mud hides my flaming face.*

"What on earth is going on?"

Colette froze at the shrill voice.

"I asked, what is going on? Will someone be kind enough to explain why my daughter is covered in mud?"

Colette turned, smiling through the mud to her mother. "Mother, how kind of you to stop by unannounced. I was just explaining the minerals of mud to the class, of course."

The boys snickered at Mrs. Fontaine's revolted expression.

Colette shot them a scowl, quieting them at once. "There was a small scuffle, but it's all sorted. Allow me to send for some tea for you while I clean up a bit."

Mother followed her up the stairs, stating her disapproval in no uncertain terms as Colette had the maid prepare a bath.

"Mother, I'll be at least a half hour. Can't we visit another time?" she called through the crack in the bathroom door as Belinda peeled off her ruined clothing.

"I'm concerned about your reputation. People are beginning to talk," her mother replied.

Clutching her robe to her neck, she poked her head through the door. "What are they saying?"

"Apparently, your own staff has been making comments that you're far too friendly with Mr. Reilly and"—she pursed her lips—"that he's an opportunist."

Colette turned to Belinda, who shrugged and mouthed it wasn't her. Sighing, she lowered herself into the rosewater as her mother listed her iniquities from the other room. After a hasty bath, Colette made herself decent while her mother continued, informing her how stories of Malcolm's low birth were circulating and that he only educated himself enough to snatch up a rich, vulnerable widow of St. Charles Avenue.

"Mr. Reilly has been nothing but a gentleman to me," she gasped, holding her wet braid out of the way as Belinda fastened the last button of her gown.

"Be that as it may, you need to preserve your reputation at any cost for the sake of the school if you want to see it succeed." Glancing at her gold watch pin, Mother rose. "Escort me to the door, dear. I'm afraid I haven't any more time to spare. I'm supposed to meet the seamstress in a quarter of an hour for a fitting for your little cotillion next month."

Leaning against the door, she groaned, relieved at her mother's departure but her head spinning at the news that could ruin everything. *Why, Lord? Why does society have to keep poking their nose in my business and forcing me to do things that aren't needed?*

"We need to get some steak on that eye," Malcolm called from the classroom, mistaking her groan for pain and not dread.

Her hand fluttered to her cheek, and she flinched upon contact. "I'm sure it's not that bad."

His brows rose, silently affirming that it was much, much worse. "I sent the twins to the kitchen with a month's worth of extra chores. And as for you, I was thinking that after a day like you've had, you and I could take a drive to the French Quarter to *Café du Monde* for some coffee and beignets to discuss how we want to handle Katie's classes for the rest of the week. We might want to inquire if Sister Joan can come and help us in Katie's absence," Malcolm suggested.

She fidgeted with the papers on her desk in their shared office space as the comments made about her relationship with "the help" flew to her mind, along with her mother's parting warning. "Thank you, but I can't as Norman will be calling tonight. However, go ahead and ask Sister Joan if she is able to come."

"That's still going on?"

Startled, she dropped an invoice. "Excuse me?"

"Sorry, I thought that since he was so, um, against the idea of your school that you would've sent him packing by now." He retrieved the bill from the floor, handing it to her.

"We've reached an understanding. Norman simply needed time to get used to the idea. He is quite supportive now." Lifting her paper, she cleared her throat. "Now, if you'll excuse me, I need to see to this bill right away." Ignoring his baffled look, she brushed past him. *I can't let any man hinder me in my work. Be it on purpose or by accident, no one shall stand in the way of my calling again.*

THANKFUL for the children's early bedtimes, Colette ducked into the schoolroom to fetch her Bible for some much-needed quiet time before her late dinner engagement with Norman, but seeing a flicker through the french doors, she stepped out onto the veranda. The delicate perfume of her favorite flower embraced her as scattered gardenia blossoms filled every surface from the door to a candlelit table where Norman stood, a bouquet of gardenias in hand.

"I remember the first time I saw you. Your hair was a bit wilder then, but your free spirit will never change." He reached out and lightly brushed her bruised cheek with his hand.

Her heart fluttered at his compliments, but she wasn't sure if it was love or if it was the scent of gardenias that clouded her mind.

"I wish I could say I've loved you from that moment, but it wasn't until I had to leave you that I knew I had lost something precious." Norman took her hand in his as he guided her to the table. "I cannot express how much I respect your work, drive, and sweet nature. My darling Colette, I think you know what I'm about to ask."

Her hands trembled as she became a girl again, crying over Norman's departure and her cold marriage that never brought her the warmth she had hoped it would.

"When I was away all of those years, I compared every woman I ever called upon to you. The way they made me laugh, or didn't. The way they looked, walked, acted.. .they all made me think of you, and I don't think I could ever be happy with anyone else."

To her surprise, the words she had longed to hear didn't cause her heart to race the way she'd imagined they would. "Norman—"

"Please, let me finish. I was a coward, afraid of marrying without money."

She sobered at the mention of money. "But, you do realize I'm dedicating my fortune to this school, to these boys, don't you?"

"Of course. I love your drive to follow the Lord's calling, but why do it alone when you can have someone by your side?" His hand wrapped about her waist. "To comfort you at night after a long day. To kiss you because you are too pretty not to be kissed." He leaned toward her, his warm breath on her lips. "Marry me."

She hadn't been kissed since she had married Robert, but she hadn't *really* been kissed since that one evening so long ago before he left. His lips pressed into hers and she waited for the electricity of old to shoot through her spine, but it felt different from before. It felt forced. She pressed her hands against his chest and gently broke their kiss as the crickets sang about them. At the sound of a window shutting, she twisted about, hoping that Malcolm had not witnessed their kiss.

Norman cupped her chin, returning her focus to him. "You don't have to answer now, but I wanted you to know that, should you choose to become my wife, I would always have your best interest at heart, no matter what."

She started to reply, but Norman rested a finger on her lips. "Sleep on it, my darling, and let me know your answer in three weeks when I return from Charleston."

CHAPTER 9

She gazed over the classroom of boys bent over their etiquette quiz. Norman's question seemed to never leave her as she weighed her options, but she knew she had to decide soon, as he expected her answer at the cotillion ball tomorrow night.

She glanced down at her sketch, which was supposed to be of Norman but had taken a very Malcolm-like turn. She added a fallen curl to the forehead, hoping it would begin to resemble Norman again. *All those years, I dreamt of Norman asking for my hand. Even when I was engaged to Robert, some part of me still hoped Norman would ride up and declare his love for me as an impediment at my wedding ceremony, saving me from a marriage of convenience. Yet even now, Norman didn't mention loving me.* She twisted her pen between her thumb and forefinger. *But, he did say that he'd support my dreams. What other motive but love would cause him to propose since he knows my fortune is going to the school? Lord, please give me some direction.*

"Mrs. Olivier?" One of the seventh-grade boys called to her with his hand raised.

She snapped her sketchbook shut. "You have a question, Jeff?"

He pointed to Julia in the door.

Giving him a nod of thanks, she scooted her chair back and crossed the room. "What's wrong?" she asked in a low voice.

"I need to talk with you"—she gave Colette a pointed stare—"about you know what. It's urgent."

Seeing as the boys had lost all concentration, she rubbed her forehead and announced, "Let's call this quiz a practice round and have an early recess, shall we?"

The boys hooted as they charged past

Julia, heading for the backyard and freedom.

Julia pressed her hands over her ears. "How do you bear such violent din? Is it possible to find a quiet spot?"

"This way." Colette led her sister up into her private parlor where they could not be overheard by little ears. "After a while, you don't notice the noise so much and it becomes more of a hum." She chuckled at Julia's horror. "If it ever *is* quiet, *then* you have a problem." She pulled the bell cord and motioned for Julia to have a seat. "So what was so urgent that you had to interrupt my class?"

Julia sank onto the settee. "You can't trust Norman."

Confused, Colette clicked the door shut. "Why would you say that when you are the one pushing me to accept his hand?"

"Yes, but I overheard him talking with Father in the study last night, and"—Julia dipped her chin—"Father requested that, once the marriage certificate is signed, Norman seize your assets."

"What?" Feeling the room spin, she sank

next to Julia. "But he promised I could keep the school."

"Which Father hopes will close in six months' time without the proper funds."

"And Norman?" She pressed her fingers to her lace jabot as Julia gave her a pained stare.

"While he didn't agree to Father's plan, he feels you will choose to close the school on your own volition when you tire of the novelty."

The breath left her lungs and she was left with one thought. "Are you sure?"

"Positive," Julia whispered, drawing her handkerchief from her sleeve. "I wish I wasn't, but it's all true."

She rose and went to the window, letting her forehead rest against the warm pane. *Well, that was quick.*

Her sister came and wrapped her arm around Colette's shoulders. "Were you so very in love with him?"

Colette gave a shaky laugh. "I'm more relieved than anything."

"What?" Julia drew back.

"Norman promised me everything I

wanted, but something was holding me back, and now I know why." Her gaze found Malcolm in the side garden, creating a raised bed for part of the agricultural class.

"Oh." Julia tucked her unused handkerchief into her reticule. "Well, I'm glad you took it so well. And it's not as if he were the only eligible bachelor who is interested in you. They've merely taken a step back out of respect for Norman." She gave Colette a peck on the cheek. "We will find you a new suitor who respects your school, never fear."

"Is it so bad that I only wish to marry again if I absolutely adore the man I am to wed? Marriage to Robert was so hard, but I know it can be wonderful." She watched as Malcolm stooped to help Darvy plant his vegetable seeds. "I know it can be sweet. I want that." She turned to Julia. "Is it too much to hope that a widow like me could have a second chance at love?"

Julia clasped her hands around Colette's. "If anyone deserves to be cherished, it's you."

"For all his faults, Norman would've tried to cherish me, but I know now that we could never make each other happy. I'm too independent for him, and he is too set in his ways for me. If I am ever to marry again, I'm going to wait for the Lord to bring me my husband. I've tried society's ways and they failed me. It's time to trust in Him with *every* aspect of my life."

At Julia's departure, Colette opened her inkwell to pen Norman a letter, thanking him for his offer but firmly refusing. Feeling no need to accuse him of scheming with her father, she signed her name with a flourish and descended the stairs to set it on the mail tray.

Hearing Luca practicing on the piano, she paused in the doorway to find that he wasn't alone. There, with the afternoon light spilling onto her beautiful, dark locks, Malcolm held Katie in his arms as they waltzed about the music room. Colette stiffened, feeling her heart drop into her stomach. She had a hard time swallowing back the lump in her throat as Malcolm stepped on Katie's hem and, giggling, she fell against his chest to avoid having her skirts ripped.

"Really, Malcolm, we've been dancing for weeks. If I didn't know any better, I would think you were *trying* to tear my skirt." Katie winked boldly at Malcolm as he righted her.

Before she could be spotted, Colette slipped into the shadows of the hallway and deposited her letter, feeling cold. *If I'm to be alone, so be it. Lord, help me bear it.*

With tears stinging and her lungs burning, she turned away, when she heard something shatter in the direction of the kitchen. Exhaling, she swiped at her cheeks and changed course to find Tommy and the twins covered in flour and Davey and Darvy fighting over the bowl of batter. "Boys! What on earth?"

Darvy silently pulled his finger from the batter, and the boys shuffled in the flour for an explanation.

"Why didn't you ask the cook for a snack if you were hungry?" She lifted her skirts to avoid the flour on the floor and reached for a clean rag to wipe off their faces.

"We wanted to surprise you—" Davey

began but stopped as Darvy elbowed him in the ribs.

"Surprise me? Well, indeed you have, but for what occasion did you want to surprise me?" She bit the inside of her mouth as she ran the rag over Darvy's face.

Relieved that she wasn't angry, Tommy shrugged. "The cotillion ball is tomorrow, so we wanted to make a chocolate cake to say sorry for almost breaking your toe five times."

The door swung open, and Ralph, the eldest boy, halted in his tracks at the sight of Colette standing in the middle of the mess. "I said to wait for me, fellows. I'm sorry, Mrs. Olivier. I guess they"—he glared at the others—"got too excited to wait while I dug up my ma's old recipe."

Her heart warmed at the boys rallying together for her. Grinning, she grabbed an apron. "Ralph, you're the teacher tonight, because my mama never let me near the stove. Let's get baking!" The Lord had seen to it that she would never be alone on this earth again.

DRESSED in a new satin cerulean gown with a low, square neck, pointed waist, and short puffed sleeves, Colette felt rather exposed after wearing such dowdy clothes in public for years, but as it was for the cotillion ball, she hoped her guests would deem it appropriate. Giving one last twirl in the ballroom looking glass, she surveyed the room, checking that everyone and everything was in its place.

Not a minute too soon, Katie brought in the boys and instructed them to stand tall in their formal wear as Mrs. Wilson heralded in the girls from her Sunday school class along with their chaperones. Colette laughed behind her fan as she watched the boys halt their fidgeting and become uncharacteristically quiet while the girls gathered on the other side of the room and the musicians began to play.

To get the dancing started, Colette and Ralph began the first waltz. The young man led her about the room with confidence, and Colette was filled with pride that he had made it through the dance without a single mishap. With a curtsy, she whispered her congratulations and pointed him in the direction of a pretty raven-haired girl.

Jumping at the touch on the small of her back, Colette turned to find Norman. "Mr. Hartley!"

"So formal." He grinned. "May I have the honor of this dance, *Mrs. Olivier*?"

She felt the blood drain from her face and glanced around for Julia, hoping her sister could save her. *Why is that girl always late?* "You wish to dance with me?"

"Please." He gave her a bow. "I've dreamed of little else during my business trip."

He didn't get the letter, she thought with horror. "Wait!"

Norman pulled her onto the dance floor. "I had thought I'd get a better welcoming than this," he teased, "all things considered."

"Norman, can we go outside and talk?" she whispered, feeling frantic as he whirled her about in the candlelight.

"Eager to kiss me again, are you?" He winked at her. "Well, you'll have to wait, little lady. I have been dying to hold you close, and as dancing is the only means of doing that until we are wed, I plan to keep you on the dance floor all evening."

The heat rushed to her cheeks as she attempted to put a little distance between them as they waltzed. "Norman. . .I know what Father asked you to do."

He missed a step and his grip tightened. "Regarding?"

"The school," her voice strained. "He asked you to consider seizing my assets."

"But I didn't agree to it," he replied, eyes wide as if he was more taken aback over being caught than ashamed of the conversation that transpired.

"But you didn't say you wouldn't," she whispered, almost apologetically. "And how can I trust a man who won't even stand up to the bullying of my own father? I sent you a note explaining everything. Didn't you get it?"

"No. I came straight from the station so as to not miss your school's debut dance." He pressed his lips into a thin line.

"May I cut in?" Malcolm tapped him on the shoulder.

At the sight of the Irishman, Norman looked as if he might begin throwing punches, but he clenched his jaw and gave her a slight bow. "Let's talk more later."

"I'm sorry," she replied, truly meaning it, "but there's nothing to discuss."

Malcolm placed a hand on her waist and waltzed her a little stiffly about the room with the rest of the class, sending the chaperones twittering behind their fluttering fans.

"I thought you said you didn't dance." Although relieved at his timing, she couldn't help but jab, still stinging from his rejection.

"I didn't, but I've been practicing in the hope that one day, I could do this"—he twirled her out onto the veranda.

"What on earth do you think you are doing?" she whispered. "We need to get back inside at once before people begin to talk."

"I heard about Norman's proposal. You can't marry him."

"That, sir, is *none* of your business." She moved to head back inside.

He took her by the elbows, turning her to him. "You can't marry him because he doesn't love you."

Is it that obvious? Hurt filled her features as she tried to pull away.

"I do," he whispered and reached out, stroking her cheek.

"What?" Her voice caught in her throat.

"I love you, Colette Olivier. Am I foolish to think you feel the same? We are from two completely different worlds, but I can't help thinking that we belong together. . .even though everyone is pushing you toward someone more suited to you." He took her hand in his. "But no one can force you to marry this time."

"What about Miss O'Dell?" she fumbled.

"Katie?"

"I saw you two dancing with only Luca as a chaperone. You didn't seem to have any trouble asking her to dance for the last few weeks." She lifted her chin.

Malcolm inhaled sharply through his teeth. "You saw that, did you?"

She gave a curt nod, disappointed he apparently had attempted to hide it from her.

"Nothing happened between us. She is seeing a close friend of mine."

"Then why—?"

"We were dancing because I felt bad that I couldn't help you in your cotillion class. I know the dances of the middle class, but your upper classes have a different way of doing things, so I asked Katie to teach me how to dance like a proper gentleman."

"Oh." She blushed, dazed by how far he went out of his way to please her.

"I love you, Colette, and I believe in our calling to raise these boys, but I don't see why we can't do it together as husband and wife. People may say I'm an opportunist, but I don't care one whit about your money. I want you to spend it all on our legacy, our boys and our school. And if you ever had doubts of me. . ." He pulled a single pink ribbon, stained on the ends with faded ink, and draped it in her palm.

She traced the ribbon. "Is this. . . ?"

"Aye. It's only ever been you in my heart, Colette," he whispered, his hands at her waist, drawing her near as the violinists began to play "Love's Old Sweet Song," its enchanting lilt floating out and enveloping them. "Say you'll be mine and let me cherish you forever."

She couldn't breathe. All she could think of was kissing this man who loved her.

"If you need to think about it, I understand," Malcolm misinterpreted her silence.

"I don't."

"Oh." His expression fell as he stepped back. "I see."

"Because I want everything you want." She closed the distance between them. "I want to love and be loved. I want someone who will treasure my boys, teach them to be men, and do anything to protect them and me. You have my hand and my heart, Malcolm Reilly." Wrapping her arms around his neck, she lifted her lips to his and lost herself in his kiss only to find the warmth and tenderness she had been dreaming of for years.

EPILOGUE

Feeling like a bride for the first time, Colette took a deep breath as she lowered her veil and accepted her wedding bouquet from Julia. Smiling so much her cheeks hurt, she descended the stairs and followed the path of rose petals out into the garden, where Malcolm waited under the giant moss-trimmed oaks.

The boys filled the chairs, and as Luca began playing the violin, they rose, their eager faces finding hers as a few hoots and hollers passed their lips. Katie shushed them, and Colette couldn't help but laugh, as she wished to shout herself. In the front row, she found her mother's supportive smile and felt the lack of her father's presence, but with time, she prayed he would come around to accepting Malcolm into the family.

Leaving all thoughts but Malcolm behind, Colette placed her hand in his and promised to be his forever.

Grace Hitchcock is the award-winning author of multiple historical novels and novellas, including the American Royalty, Best Laid Plans, and Aprons & Veils series. She holds a Master's in Creative Writing and a Bachelor of Arts in English with a minor in History. Grace lives in South Louisiana with her husband, Dakota, sons, and daughter in a farmhouse that is always filled with the sounds of sweet little footsteps running at full speed. When not writing, chasing her toddlers, or tending to her chickens and golden and British labrador retrievers, she's baking something delightful and can usually be found with a book clutched in her fist.

More in your favorite series . . .

Forced into a betrothal with a widower twice her age, Charleston socialite, Sophia Fairfield is desperate for an escape. Much to her dismay, Sophia finds herself falling in love with the wrong gentleman—a man society would never allow her to marry, given Sophia was supposed to be his new stepmother. The only way to save Carver from ruin is to run away, leaving him and all else behind to become a Harvey Girl waitress at the Castañeda Hotel in New Mexico.

The Finding of Miss Fairfield by Grace Hitchcock
Aprons & Veils #1
A Friends-to-Lovers Runaway Bride RomCom

With a hope for belonging, Belle Parish leaves her position as a maid in Charleston to travel to New Mexico to become a mail-order bride. Colt Lawson's letters hold great promise, but something does not add up. Belle flees straight into the Castañeda Hotel Harvey House. Giving up the prospect of marrying, she focuses on her role as a Harvey Girl waitress until a strong Texas Ranger rides into her life.

The Pursuit of Miss Parish by Grace Hitchcock
Aprons & Veils #2
A Mail-Order Bride RomCom

Tanner Sterling has hunted his last bounty. As a new foreman, he wasn't expecting to rescue a sweet Harvey Girl from a raging river his first day. But, when he sees her on a wanted poster, he knows hunters will be coming for her. Despite wanting to hang up his past along with his gun belt, Tanner will do anything to protect her from the coming storm . . . even if he has to claim the bounty himself.

The Vanishing of Miss Victoria by Grace Hitchcock
Aprons & Veils #4
An Enemies-to-Lovers RomCom

You May Also Like . . .

Upon her father's unexpected retirement, his shareholders refuse to allow Willow Dupré to take over the company without a man at her side. Presented with thirty potential suitors from New York society's elite, she has six months to choose which she will marry. But when one captures her heart, she must discover for herself if his motives are truly pure.

My Dear Miss Dupré by Grace Hitchcock
AMERICAN ROYALTY #1
GraceHitchcock.com

A very public jilting has Theodore Day fleeing the ballrooms of New York to focus on building his family's luxury steamboat business in New Orleans and beating out his brother to be next in charge. But he can't escape the Southern belles' notice, nor Flora Wingfield, who is determined to win his attention.

Her Darling Mr. Day by Grace Hitchcock
AMERICAN ROYALTY #2
GraceHitchcock.com

After years of being her diva mother's understudy, it's time for Delia Vittoria to take her place on stage. Attempting to make amends for a grave mistake, Kit Quincy is suddenly pulled into Delia's plot to win the great opera war and act as her patron and an enigmatic phantom. But when a second phantom appears, more than Delia's career is threatened.

His Delightful Lady Delia by Grace Hitchcock
AMERICAN ROYALTY #3
GraceHitchcock.com

Sign Up for Grace's Newsletter!

Keep up to date with Grace's news on book releases and giveaways by signing up for her email list at GraceHitchcock.com

More from Grace Hitchcock

Forced into a betrothal with a widower twice her age, Charleston socialite, Sophia Fairfield is desperate for an escape. But, while her fiancé is away on business, he assigns his handsome stepson, Carver, the task of looking after his bride-to-be. Much to her dismay, Sophia finds herself falling in love with the wrong gentleman—a man society would never allow her to marry, given Sophia was supposed to be his new stepmother. The only way to save Carver from scandal and financial ruin is to run away, leaving him and all else behind to become a Harvey Girl waitress at the Castañeda Hotel in New Mexico.

The Finding of Miss Fairfield by Grace Hitchcock
APRONS & VEILS #1
GraceHitchcock.com

www.ingramcontent.com/pod-product-compliance
Lightning Source LLC
LaVergne TN
LVHW091004080826
845145LV00003B/1117